Volume

Cups (US)	US fl. oz / pints	Metric	Metric	Imperial	Cups (UK)
1 tsp		5 ml	5 ml		1 tsp
1 tbsp	½ fl. oz	15 ml	15 ml	½ fl. oz	1 tbsp
	⅔ fl. oz	20 ml	20 ml	⅔ fl. oz	1 Aus tbsp
2 tbsp	1 fl. oz	30 ml	30 ml	1 fl. oz	2 tbsp
¼ cup	2 fl. oz	60 ml	60 ml	2 fl. oz	¼ cup
⅓ cup	2 ¾ fl. oz	80 ml	80 ml	2 ¾ fl. oz	⅓ cup
	3 fl. oz	90 ml	85 ml	3 fl. oz	
½ cup	¼ pint	120 ml	120 ml	4 ¼ fl. oz	½ cup
	5 fl. oz	150 ml	150 ml	¼ pint	
⅔ cup	5 ½ fl. oz	160 ml	160 ml	5 ⅔ fl. oz	⅔ cup
¾ cup	6 fl. oz	180 ml	180 ml	6 ⅓ fl. oz	¾ cup
	6 ¾ fl. oz	200 ml	200 ml	7 fl. oz	
1 cup	½ pint	240 ml	240 ml	8 ½ fl. oz	1 cup
1 ¼ cups	10 fl. oz	300 ml	300 ml	10 ½ fl. oz	1 ¼ cups
1 ½ cups	12 fl. oz	355 ml	360 ml	12 ⅔ fl. oz	1 ½ cups
1 ¾ cups	14 fl. oz	415 ml	420 ml	¾ pint	1 ¾ cups
2 cups	1 pint	475 ml	480 ml	17 fl. oz	2 cups
2 ½ cups	1 ¼ pints	590 ml	600 ml	1 pint	2 ½ cups
3 cups	1 ½ pints	710 ml	720 ml	1 ¼ pints	3 cups
3 ½ cups	1 ¾ pints	830 ml	840 ml	1 ½ pints	3 ½ cups
4 cups	2 pints	950 ml	960 ml		4 cups

Butter

Spoons	Sticks	Cups	Imperial	Metric
1 tbsp				
2 tbsp	¼ stick		1 oz	28 g
3 tbsp				
4 tbsp	½ stick	¼ cup	2 oz	57 g
5 tbsp		⅓ cup		
6 tbsp	¾ stick		3 oz	85 g
7 tbsp				
8 tbsp	1 stick	½ cup	4 oz	113 g

The great fairy baking competition

make believe ideas

Welcome to the great fairy baking competition

Camilla the Cupcake Fairy and her friends love to bake cakes and treats for each other. Once a year they get together for the biggest contest in Fairyland – the great fairy baking competition!

Inside this special book you will find each fairy's favorite recipes. All the recipes will be entered into the competition – which one do you think will win first prize?

Camilla the Cupcake Fairy

Camilla is Fairyland's youngest fairy. She is five years old and has a special wand that makes toppings for cupcakes. Her best friends are Maya and Molly.

Camilla

Molly

Maya

Daisy

Daisy the Donut Fairy

Daisy lives with her sisters, Dee and Dolly, in a lighthouse made of donuts! They love to bake donuts but have some other special recipes they'd love to share!

Dolly

Dee

Lola the Lollipop Fairy

Lola and her sisters, Lulu and Linda, star in a famous circus show. They think cake tastes best when you eat it off a stick – just like a lollipop!

Lola

Linda

Lulu

Izzy

Mo

Mia

Izzy the Ice-cream Fairy

Izzy and her special friends, Mo and Mia, live on a beautiful beach next to a magical ice-cream well! Izzy's recipes are perfect for hot, sunny days.

Annie the Apple Pie Fairy

Annie has her own TV show, and she is a Fairyland family favorite. She loves baking pies most of all. Her best friends are Pip and Cora.

Cora

Pip

Annie

Katie the Candy Cane Fairy

Katie is a singer who performs in a magical Christmas show with her friends, Crystal and Glo. They love anything with stripes – especially candy canes! Katie's bakes make delicious Christmas treats.

Katie

Glo

Crystal

Be careful!

Follow Camilla's easy kitchen rules and you will make sure that baking time is always magical!

Get ready!

♥ Wash and dry your hands before you do anything. Nobody wants your germs!

♥ If you have long hair like Katie the Candy Cane Fairy, tie it back so it doesn't fall in your food!

♥ Put on an apron to keep your clothes nice and clean.

Get organized!

♥ Clear plenty of space to work.

♥ Find all the equipment you need and put it all together in one place.

♥ Measure out all the ingredients you need and put them aside.

Get going!

♥ Follow the recipe carefully.

♥ Knives can be dangerous. Always ask an adult to help with cutting and slicing.

♥ Never touch anything electrical with wet hands.

♥ Always keep pan handles turned to the side so they cannot be knocked over as you walk by.

♥ When using the oven or handling anything hot, always wear oven mitts or use a pot holder, and ask an adult to help you.

Contents

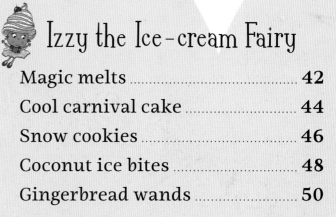
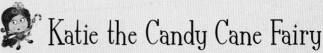

What you need

Here are all the things Camilla and her friends use to make perfect cakes and treats!

measuring cups

measuring spoons

scale

whisk

hand whisk

wooden spoon

knife

palette knife

fork

sharp knife

pastry brush

cutting board

rolling pin

icing bag

flour sifter

strainer

cupcake tray

baking sheet

square baking tin

baking cups

round and fluted
cookie cutters

star-shaped
cookie cutters

heart-shaped
cookie cutters

foil

wax paper

popsicle sticks

lollipop sticks

plastic wrap

ziplock bag

wire rack

mixing bowls

plate

microwave-safe bowls

glass

saucepan

donut pan

giant cupcake tin

loaf tin

round cake tin

Baking basics

Here are some kitchen tips that will be useful when you start baking!

Cracking eggs

1. Gently tap the middle of an egg on the side of a bowl, so that the shell cracks.

2. Using your fingers, pull the halves apart, letting the yolk and white fall into the bowl. Discard the shell.

3. Remove any shell from the bowl using the wrong end of a teaspoon.

Separating eggs

1. Crack the egg open, holding the two shell halves up like cups to catch the yolk.

2. Let the egg white fall into one bowl, then tip the egg yolk back and forth between the halves until any remaining egg white has fallen out.

3. Drop the egg yolk into another bowl.

Beating eggs

Light: Whisk until the mixture is completely yellow.

Soft peaks: Whisk the egg whites at high speed for 2 minutes with an electric mixer or for up to 10 minutes with a hand whisk, until the mixture forms peaks that curl down when you remove the whisk.

Stiff peaks: Whisk the egg whites at high speed for up to 4 minutes with an electric mixer or for 10–15 minutes with a hand whisk, until the mixture forms peaks that do not move even when you tilt the bowl.

Rolling out

1. Make sure your surface is clean and dry. Sift flour (for dough and pastry) or powdered sugar (for icing) lightly onto the surface and rub over the rolling pin to prevent sticking.

2. Roll dough, pastry, or icing into a ball shape. If the dough mixture falls apart, add a few drops of water to stick it together.

3. Place the ball on the floured surface and roll out with the rolling pin. Keep rolling the dough, pastry, or icing until it is about ¼ in (3 mm) thick.

4. Cut out shapes with a cookie cutter. When you cannot cut out any more, gather the scraps into a ball and repeat steps 2 and 3. Use a palette knife to help you lift up the cut-out shapes if they are sticking.

Making breadcrumbs

1. Wash your hands with cold water and dry them thoroughly.

2. Sift flour into a bowl.

3. Cut butter into small cubes and add it to the bowl.

4. Using your fingertips, rub the butter into the flour until no large lumps of butter remain and the mix looks like breadcrumbs.

Preparing fruit

1. Wash the fruit thoroughly in the sink.

2. Cut off any stems – for strawberries, run a knife around the stalk to cut out a little of the core, and for apples, carefully peel the skin with a sharp knife.

3. Cut into roughly ¼ in (5 mm) cubes with a sharp knife.

Mashed: Put the chunks in a bowl and mash with a fork.

Puréed: Push the mashed mixture through a large strainer.

Melting chocolate

1. Break the chocolate into small chunks and put in a microwave-safe bowl.

2. Microwave the chocolate for 60 seconds, then take it out and stir it with a spoon.

3. If the chocolate has not fully melted, put it back in the microwave for another 10 seconds. Keep doing this until you can stir out any remaining lumps.

Warning: Do not overcook as this will burn the chocolate!

11

Fairy cupcakes

Makes 12

You will need

cupcake tray
12 baking cups
measuring cups / scale
large bowl
whisk
sifter
wooden spoon
teaspoon
wire rack

3 medium eggs
♥
1 ½ cups / 5 ⅓ oz / 150 g
all-purpose flour
♥
1 ½ tsp baking powder
♥
⅓ tsp salt
♥
1 ⅓ stick / 5 ⅓ oz / 150 g
unsalted butter
♥
¾ cup / 5 ⅓ oz / 150 g
superfine sugar

1

Beat the eggs in a bowl.

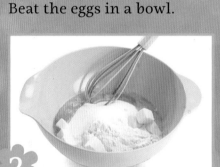

2

Sift the flour, baking powder and salt into the bowl, add the butter and sugar, and mix for about 2 minutes until creamy.

3

Use a teaspoon to put a little mixture into each baking cup so it is about ¾ full. Bake the cakes in the oven for about 15 minutes until they are golden brown.

"Cool the cakes on a wire rack."

12

Fancy frosting

Serves **12**

You will need

measuring cups / scale
measuring spoons
large bowl
sifter
wooden spoon
knife / icing bag

2 cups / 8 ¾ oz / 250 g
powdered sugar

♥

½ cup / 4 ½ oz / 125 g
unsalted butter

♥

2 tbsp milk

♥

2 drops vanilla extract

1 Sift the powdered sugar into a bowl.

*Instead of milk and vanilla extract, use the instructions below for other exciting buttercream flavors!

2 Add the butter and mix with a wooden spoon, then add the milk and vanilla (or a flavor of your choice*) and mix until smooth.

To decorate your cake, put 2 tsp buttercream on top of the cupcake, swirl it around with a knife or the back of a spoon (or use an icing bag), then add your favorite sprinkles.

3

Lemon zing buttercream:
Mix 2 drops yellow food coloring, 1 tsp grated lemon rind, and 2 tsp lemon juice into the buttercream.

Raspberry buttercream:
Mix 3 tbsp raspberry jam into the buttercream.

Chocolate buttercream:
Mix 3 tbsp chocolate spread into the buttercream.

Banana caramel buttercream:
Mix sliced banana and 3 tbsp caramel syrup together, then stir into the buttercream.

"Try these delicious flavors."

Powdered sugar icing

♥ 1 cup / 4 ½ oz / 125 g powdered sugar

♥ 1 tbsp warm water

♥ 2 drops food coloring

Sift powdered sugar into a bowl. Add water, a few drops at a time, until all the powdered sugar is absorbed but the mixture is still thick enough to coat the back of a spoon.* For colored icing, add food coloring and stir.

*Add a little more powdered sugar for piping.

Strawberry surprise

Preheat the oven to 350°F / 180°C and put the baking cups in the cupcake tray.

Makes 12

You will need

cupcake tray
12 baking cups
measuring cups / scale
measuring spoons
large bowl
whisk
sifter
wooden spoon
teaspoon
wire rack

1 batch / 1 lb 5 oz / 600 g
cupcake mixture (see p12)

♥

½ cup / 3 ½ oz / 100 g
white chocolate chips

♥

1 ⅓ cups / 7 oz / 200 g
chopped strawberries

♥

½ cup / 1 ¾ oz / 50 g
white chocolate curls

1 Make the cupcake mixture in a bowl.

2 Stir in the chocolate chips and ¾ of the strawberries.

3 Spoon the mixture into the baking cups, then bake for about 15 minutes until golden brown.

"Cool the cakes on a wire rack."

14

"Decorate with fresh strawberries and white chocolate curls."

Chocolate delights

Preheat the oven to 350°F / 180°C and put the baking cups in the cupcake tray.

Makes 12

You will need

cupcake tray

12 baking cups

measuring cups / scale

measuring spoons

large bowl

whisk

sifter

wooden spoon

teaspoon

wire rack

medium bowl

1 batch / 1 lb 5 oz / 600 g
cupcake mixture (see p12)

♥

3 tbsp
cocoa powder

♥

1 batch / 14 oz / 400 g
chocolate buttercream
(see p13)

♥

½ cup / 3 ½ oz / 100 g
chocolate wafers

♥

4 cups / 7 oz / 200 g
mini marshmallows

♥

1 tbsp powdered sugar

1

Make the cupcake mixture in a bowl, then add the cocoa and mix well.

2

Spoon the mixture into the baking cups, bake for about 15 minutes, then cool on a wire rack.

3

Ice the cakes with chocolate buttercream, chocolate wafers, and mini marshmallows.

"Dust the finished cakes with powdered sugar."

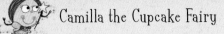

Fairy flutter cakes

Preheat the oven to 350°F / 180°C and put the baking cups in the cupcake tray.

Makes 12

You will need

cupcake tray

12 baking cups

measuring cups / scale

measuring spoons

large bowl

whisk

sifter

wooden spoon

teaspoon

wire rack

knife

medium bowl

1 batch / 1 lb 5 oz / 600 g cupcake mixture (see p12)

♥

½ cup / 3⅓ fl. oz / 100 ml honey

♥

1 batch / 14 oz / 400 g buttercream (see p13)

♥

2 tbsp pink sprinkles

♥

1 tbsp powdered sugar

1 Make the cupcake mixture in a bowl.

2 Stir 3 ½ tsp honey into the mixture.

3 Spoon the mixture into the cups, bake for about 15 minutes until golden brown, then cool on a wire rack.

4 Cut out a shallow dip in the center of a cake, cut the removed piece in half, and leave it to one side.

5 Put 1 tsp honey into the dip, then put 2 tsp buttercream on top of the honey and spread it over the cake.

6 Put the cut-out pieces back on top of the cake, sticking out like fairy wings, and add some sprinkles.

"Drizzle honey over your cakes and dust them with powdered sugar."

19

Giant cupcake

Serves
16

You will need

giant cupcake tin*

measuring cups / scale

measuring spoons

large bowl

sifter

whisk

wooden spoon

wire rack

medium bowl

icing bag

*Alternatively use 3 cake tins
(see Treasure island p30).

1 tbsp unsalted butter

♥

4 cups / 14 oz / 400 g
all-purpose flour

♥

3 ¾ tsp baking powder

♥

1 ½ tsp salt

♥

8 medium eggs
(lightly beaten)

♥

3 ½ sticks / 14 oz / 400 g
unsalted butter

♥

2 cups / 14 oz / 400 g sugar

♥

2 drops vanilla extract

♥

2 batches/ 1 lb 12 oz / 800 g
buttercream (see p13)

♥

1 cup / 7 oz / 200 g
sprinkles / candies

Preheat the oven
to 350°F / 180°C
and grease the tin
with butter.

Sift the flour, baking powder,
and salt into a bowl, add the
eggs, butter, sugar, and
vanilla and mix for about
2 minutes until it is creamy.

Put the mixture into the tin
and bake for 20 minutes
until golden brown, then
cool on a wire rack.

Put the cake together,
then cover it with piped
buttercream.

"Decorate
with your choice of
candies."

20

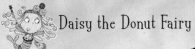

Rockin' rock cakes

Makes 6

You will need

baking sheet

wax paper

measuring cups / scale

large bowl

wooden spoon

tablespoon

wire rack

Preheat the oven to 375°F / 190°C and grease the sheet with butter or line with wax paper.

¾ cup / 3 oz / 85 g
all-purpose flour

♥

1 ¼ tsp baking powder

♥

¼ tsp salt

♥

½ stick / 1 ¾ oz / 50 g
unsalted butter

♥

1 small egg

♥

¼ cup / 1 ½ oz / 45 g
sugar

♥

¼ cup / 1 ¼ oz / 35 g
raisins

♥

¼ cup / 1 ¼ oz / 35 g chopped
maraschino cherries

♥

¼ cup / 1 ¼ oz / 35 g
chocolate chips

1 Mix the flour, baking powder, salt, and butter until it has the consistency of breadcrumbs.

2 Stir in the egg, sugar, raisins, cherries, and chocolate chips.

3 Put large spoonfuls of the mix onto the sheet. Don't smooth them out, as you want them to look like rocks. Bake for 15–20 minutes until they are golden brown.

"Cool the cakes on a wire rack."

Donut dinghies

Makes 10

You will need

donut pan

measuring cups / scale

measuring spoons

large bowl

sifter

wooden spoon

teaspoon

wire rack

microwave-safe bowl

spoon

2 tsp unsalted butter

♥

1 ½ cups / 5 ⅓ oz / 150 g
all-purpose flour

♥

1 tsp baking powder

♥

¼ tsp salt

♥

2 medium eggs

♥

2 tbsp cooking oil

♥

½ cup / 3 ½ oz / 100 g
sugar

♥

1 cup / 6 ¾ fl. oz / 200 ml
buttermilk

♥

⅔ cup / 3 ½ oz / 100 g
raspberries

♥

½ cup / 3 ½ oz / 100 g
white baking chocolate

1 Sift the flour, baking powder, and salt into a bowl.

2 Add the eggs, oil, sugar, and buttermilk and mix until smooth.

3 Stir in the raspberries.

4 Spoon the mix into the pan, bake for 15–20 minutes until golden brown, then cool on a wire rack.

5 Melt the chocolate, then drizzle over the donuts and leave to set.

"A delicious seaside snack!"

Sparkly starfish

Makes 8

You will need

baking sheet
wax paper
measuring cups / scale
measuring spoons
large bowl
wooden spoon
rolling pin
star-shaped cookie cutter
wire rack
knife
microwave-safe bowl
spoon

Preheat the oven to 375°F / 190°C and line the baking sheet with wax paper.

1 ½ cups / 5 ⅓ oz / 150 g all-purpose flour
♥
7 tbsp / 3 ½ oz / 100 g unsalted butter
♥
¼ cup / 1 ¾ oz / 50 g sugar
♥
1 lb / 500 g white fondant icing
♥
3 tbsp powdered sugar icing (see p13)
♥
½ cup / 3 ½ oz / 100 g white baking chocolate
♥
2 tbsp sprinkles

1 Breadcrumb the flour and butter, add the sugar and mix.

2 Shape the mixture into a ball and roll out the dough on a floured surface.

"Use different colored **sprinkles** to make your **starfish shimmer!**"

3 Cut out shapes using the cutter and put them on the sheet. Bake for 15–18 minutes, leave to harden for 2 minutes, then cool on a wire rack.

4 Roll out the icing and cut out stars for the top of the cookies.

5 Put a dab of powdered sugar icing on the top of a cookie and stick the icing star to it.

6 Add some melted white chocolate and decorate with sprinkles.

Swirly slices

Makes
15

You will need

baking sheet
(1 in / 2–3 cm deep)

wax paper

measuring cups / scale

measuring spoons

saucepan

ziplock bag

rolling pin

wooden spoon

microwave-safe bowl

spoon

knife

1 stick / 4 oz / 110g
unsalted butter

♥

2 tbsp sugar

♥

2 tbsp honey

♥

4 tsp cocoa powder

♥

8 oz / 225 g
crunchy chocolate
chip cookies

♥

⅔ cup / 3 ½ oz / 100 g
raisins

♥

1 ¼ cups / 8 oz / 225 g
baking chocolate
(mix of dark and milk)

♥

½ cup / 3 ½ oz / 100 g
white baking chocolate

Line the baking
sheet with
wax paper.

1 Put the butter, sugar, honey, and cocoa in a saucepan and melt over a low heat.

2 Put the cookies in a ziplock bag and crush into small chunks with a rolling pin.

3 Add the cookies and raisins to the saucepan and mix together well.

4 Put the mixture into the sheet and push it down with the back of a spoon.

5 Melt the chocolate and pour it out so that the mix is completely covered, then drizzle white chocolate over the top. Refrigerate for about 2 hours, then take it out of the sheet, place it on a board, and cut into squares.

"These are **best** served cold."

Treasure island

Serves
16

You will need

4 round cake tins

wax paper

measuring cups / scale

measuring spoons

large bowl

sifter

whisk

wooden spoon

wire rack

plate

knife

4 cups / 14 oz / 400 g
all-purpose flour

♥

3 ¾ tsp baking powder

♥

1 ½ tsp salt

♥

8 medium eggs
(lightly beaten)

♥

3 ½ sticks / 14 oz / 400 g
unsalted butter

♥

2 drops vanilla extract

♥

2 cups / 14 oz / 400 g
sugar

♥

2 batches / 1 lb 8 oz / 800 g
buttercream (see p13)

♥

7 oz / 200 g
bag of mixed candies

Preheat the oven to
350°F / 180°C and
line the cake tins
with wax paper.

1 Sift the flour, baking powder, and salt into a bowl, add the eggs, butter, vanilla extract, and sugar and mix for about 2 minutes until it is creamy.

2 Divide the mixture evenly into the cake tins and bake for 15–20 minutes until golden brown, then cool on a wire rack.

3 Place the first cake on a plate and cover with buttercream. Place the remaining 3 cakes on top of the first, with layers of buttercream between them.

4 Ice the sides and top of the layered cake and decorate it with candies.

"A fun idea for a birthday cake!"

Lola the Lollipop Fairy

Cutest cake pops

Line a baking sheet with wax paper and half-fill a glass with sugar.

Makes **12**

You will need

baking sheet
wax paper
glass
measuring cups / scale
measuring spoons
large bowl
wooden spoon
12 lollipop sticks
microwave-safe bowl
spoon

6 cupcakes (see p12)
♥
½ cup / 3 ½ oz / 100 g buttercream (see p13)
♥
2 ¼ cups / 14 oz / 400 g baking chocolate
♥
2 tbsp sprinkles

1 In a bowl, break up the cupcakes until they look like breadcrumbs, then mix in the buttercream.

2 Using your hands, squeeze the mixture into 1 in (2 cm) balls, put them on the sheet, then freeze for 30 minutes.

3 Push a lollipop stick into the center of each cake pop.

4 Melt the chocolate. Take the stick out of each pop, dip the end into the chocolate, then put the stick back in. This will hold it in place.

5 Put the pops in the freezer for another 5 minutes, then dip them into the melted chocolate, making sure they are completely covered.

6 Shake any drips back into the bowl, wait 5 seconds, then dip the pops in the sprinkles. Stand the pops in a glass and cool them in the fridge.

Happy heart pops

Line a baking sheet with wax paper and half-fill a glass with sugar.

Makes 6

You will need

8 x 8 in (20 x 20 cm) baking sheet

wax paper

glass

measuring cups / scale

measuring spoons

saucepan

wooden spoon

2 ½ in (6 cm) heart-shaped cookie cutter

6 lollipop sticks

microwave-safe bowl

spoon

---

1 ¾ tbsp / 1 oz / 25 g unsalted butter

♥

1 cup / 7 oz / 200 g white baking chocolate

♥

4 ½ oz / 125 g / approx. 16 jumbo marshmallows

♥

2 drops pink food coloring

♥

4 ⅔ cups / 3 ½ oz / 100 g toasted rice cereal

♥

2 tbsp sprinkles

1 Melt the butter and half the chocolate in a saucepan over a low heat.

2 Add the marshmallows and food coloring and stir until they have melted.

3 Remove the pan from the heat, add the cereal, and stir.

"Perfect for parties and sharing with friends."

4

Spoon the mixture into the sheet and spread it with the back of the spoon, then leave it to cool for 10–15 minutes.

5

Cut out heart shapes with the cutter, and then push a stick into the bottom of each heart.

6

Melt the remaining chocolate and drizzle it over the hearts, decorate with sprinkles, and stand in the glass.

Marshmallow disco pops

Half-fill a glass with sugar.

Makes 6

You will need

glass
baking sheet
measuring cups / scale
measuring spoons
6 lollipop sticks
microwave-safe bowl
spoon

6 jumbo marshmallows
♥
1 cup / 7 oz / 200 g
white baking chocolate
♥
2 tbsp sprinkles

36

" To make multi-colored disco pops, try adding food coloring to the melted chocolate. "

1

Put the marshmallows on a sheet. Push a lollipop stick into each marshmallow, then freeze for 10 minutes.

2

Melt the chocolate, then dip each marshmallow so it is completely covered.

3

Wait for 5 seconds, then dip the pop in the sprinkles and stand it in the glass to dry.

4

For an edible disco ball, stick the marshmallows on cocktail sticks, then push them into a styrofoam ball.

Cookie pops

Half-fill 6 glasses with sugar, sprinkles, or candies.

Makes 6

You will need

6 glasses
tray
measuring cups / scale
measuring spoons
6 lollipop sticks
microwave-safe bowl
spoon

6 cream-centered cookies
♥
1 cup / 7 oz / 200 g
white, plain, or milk
baking chocolate
♥
2 tbsp sprinkles

1 Put the cookies on a tray. Push a lollipop stick into the cream center of each cookie, then freeze for 5 minutes.

2 Melt the chocolate, then take the cookies from the freezer and dip them into the chocolate until they are completely covered.

3 Shake any drips back into the bowl, wait for 5 seconds, then dip the pops into the sprinkles.

"Try standing the lollipops in glass jars filled with sprinkles."

Banutty wands

Half-fill 6 glasses with sugar or candies.

Makes 6

You will need

6 glasses
measuring cups / scale
cutting board
knife
6 popsicle sticks
microwave-safe bowl
spoon
tray / bowl

---

3 small bananas

♥

1 cup / 6 oz / 175 g
smooth peanut butter

♥

2 ⅓ cups / 1 ¾ oz / 50 g
lightly crushed
puffed-wheat cereal

1 Peel and cut the bananas into chunks about 2 in (5 cm) long. Push a stick into the bottom of each chunk.

2 Put the peanut butter in a bowl and microwave for 10–15 seconds, so it is melted but not too runny, and stir. Dip the wands in the bowl so they are completely covered.

3 Put the crushed cereal on a tray or in a bowl and roll the bananas in it, before standing the wands in the glasses.

"Display your wands in jars or even cute flowerpots!"

Magic melts

Makes 6

You will need

2 baking sheets
wax paper
measuring cups / scale
measuring spoons
large bowl
hand whisk
3 small bowls
spoon
icing bag
+ ½ in (1.25 cm) tip

3 large eggs

♥

¼ tsp salt

♥

1 cup / 6 oz / 175 g
superfine sugar

♥

2–3 drops
different food colorings

Preheat the oven to 275°F / 140°C and line the baking sheets with wax paper.

1 Separate the eggs and discard the yolks. Add the salt to the egg white and whisk until stiff. Then add the sugar, 1 tablespoon at a time, while mixing.

2 When the mixture is stiff and glossy, separate it into 3 small bowls. Add different food coloring to each bowl and stir.

3 Fill the icing bag and pipe out shapes, rinsing the bag between each color, or simply spoon the mix onto the sheet. Bake for 45–50 minutes, swapping the sheets around after 25 minutes.

4 When the meringues are crisp on top, turn off the oven. Open the door slightly and leave the meringues inside for an hour.

5 When the meringues have cooled, make them into sandwiches using frozen yogurt, buttercream, or ice cream.

Izzy the Ice-cream Fairy

Cool carnival cake

Line the tin with plastic wrap so the wrap overlaps the edges.

Serves
8

You will need

loaf tin

plastic wrap

measuring cups / scale

measuring spoons

large bowl

electric hand whisk

spoon

medium bowl

microwave-safe bowl

---

16 lady fingers

♥

1 ¼ cups / 8 fl. oz / 250 ml
sweetened condensed milk

♥

¾ cup / 6 ⅔ fl. oz / 200 ml
heavy whipping cream

♥

½ tsp vanilla extract

♥

⅔ cup / ¼ pint / 150 ml milk

♥

2 drops
pink food coloring

♥

¼ cup / 1 ¼ oz / 35 g
mashed strawberries

♥

¼ cup / 1 ¾ oz / 50 g
white baking chocolate

♥

2 tbsp pink sprinkles

1 Place 8 lady fingers in the tin at intervals so they stand up around the side, then set the tin aside.

2 In a large bowl, whisk the condensed milk, cream, and vanilla extract until the mixture is stiff.

3 Slowly add the milk and continue whisking until it is very stiff, then spoon half the mix into the loaf tin.

4 Mix the food coloring and strawberries into the other half of the mix and spoon it on top of the white mix.

5 Lay the rest of the lady fingers along the top. Freeze for 4 hours or until the cream is completely frozen.

6 Turn the tin upside-down onto a plate and remove the tin and plastic wrap. Drizzle melted white chocolate over the top.

44

"Decorate your cake with **pink** sprinkles!"

Izzy the Ice-cream Fairy

Snow Cookies

Preheat the oven to 400°F / 200°C and line a baking sheet with wax paper.

Makes **24**

You will need

baking sheet
wax paper
measuring cups / scale
measuring spoons
large bowl
wooden spoon
sifter
wire rack

1 ¼ stick / 4 ½ oz / 125 g
unsalted butter
♥
½ cup / 3 ½ oz / 100 g
light brown sugar
♥
1 medium egg
(lightly beaten)
♥
1 ½ tsp vanilla extract
♥
2 ½ cups / 8 ¾ oz / 250 g
all-purpose flour
♥
1 ½ tsp baking powder
♥
¾ tsp salt
♥
1 cup / 7 oz / 200 g
white chocolate chips
♥
1 tbsp powdered sugar

1 Put the butter and sugar in a large bowl and mix, then add the egg and vanilla extract.

2 Sift the flour, baking powder, and salt, then add the chocolate chips and mix.

3 Roll the dough into ¾ in (2 cm) balls. Put the balls onto the sheet, flatten them with your palm, and make sure they are spaced out.

"Bake for 12-15 minutes until golden."

"Cool the cookies on a wire rack, then dust with **powdered sugar.**"

"These cookies are **delicious** with your favorite **milkshake.**"

47

Coconut ice bites

Line a baking tin with foil.

Makes **16**

You will need

8 x 8 in (20 x 20 cm) baking tin

foil

measuring cups / scale

sifter

large bowl

wooden spoon

2 medium bowls

spoon

cutting board

knife

2 cups / 8 ¾ oz / 250 g powdered sugar

♥

1 cup / 6 ¾ fl. oz / 200 ml sweetened condensed milk

♥

3 ⅓ cups / 8 ¾ oz / 250 g shredded coconut

♥

4–6 drops pink food coloring

"Ask an adult to help you stir as the mixture will be very stiff."

1 Sift a spoonful of powdered sugar into the foil-lined tin.

2 Sift the rest of the powdered sugar into a bowl. Add the milk and coconut then beat together.

"Put the tin in the **fridge** for **3** hours. When it is **firm**, turn it out onto a board, remove the foil, and cut into **squares**."

3 Divide the mixture into 2 bowls. Add food coloring to one bowl and mix well.

4 Spoon the pink mix into the tin and spread it evenly. Then spoon the white coconut mix on top and smooth flat.

Gingerbread wands

Preheat the oven to 350°F / 180°C and line a baking sheet with wax paper.

Makes 6

You will need

baking sheet

wax paper

measuring cups / scale

measuring spoons

large bowl

wooden spoon

sifter

teaspoon

rolling pin

star-shaped cookie cutter

6 lollipop sticks

½ stick / 1 ¾ oz / 50 g unsalted butter

♥

2 tbsp brown sugar

♥

2 tbsp molasses

♥

½ tsp baking soda

♥

1 cup / 3 ½ oz / 100 g all-purpose flour

♥

1 tsp ground ginger

♥

1 tsp cinnamon

♥

½ tsp ground nutmeg

♥

2 tbsp powdered sugar icing

♥

2 tbsp sprinkles

1 In a large bowl, mix the butter and sugar, then add the molasses.

2 Sift the baking soda and flour, add the ginger, cinnamon, and nutmeg, and mix.

3 Form a ball with the dough and then roll out.

4 Cut out star shapes and place them on the sheet.

"Decorate with your choice of **icing** and **sprinkles."**

5 Bake for 10–12 minutes until golden brown. As soon as they come out of the oven, push a lollipop stick into each star to make a wand.

Apple puffs

Preheat the oven to 400°F / 200°C and line a baking sheet with wax paper.

Makes 10

You will need

baking sheet

wax paper

measuring cups / scale

measuring spoons

rolling pin

4 in (10 cm) round cookie cutter

medium bowl

wooden spoon

teaspoon

pastry brush

fork

knife

wire rack

1 tbsp all-purpose flour

♥

12 ⅓ oz / 350 g ready-made puff pastry

♥

⅔ cup / 3 ½ oz / 100 g mashed blackberries

♥

1 large eating apple, finely chopped

♥

¼ cup / 1 ¾ oz / 50 g sugar

♥

1 tbsp water

♥

1 tbsp milk

Sprinkle a surface with flour, roll the pastry, then cut out 10 circles with the cutter.

Mix the blackberries, apple, and half the sugar.

Put 1 teaspoon of the mix on one side of each circle, then brush around the edge of the pastry with water.

Now fold each pastry circle in half so they look like half-moons and press the edges down with a fork.

Brush the top of the moons with a little milk and sprinkle sugar on top. Using a knife, cut a cross shape in the top of the pastry.

"Bake the puffs for 20-30 minutes until golden brown, then cool them on a wire rack."

"Serve the puffs hot with ice cream."

Apple snackles

Preheat the oven to 375°F / 190°C and line a baking sheet with wax paper.

Makes 8

You will need

4 x 6 in (10 x 15 cm) baking sheet

wax paper

measuring cups / scale

measuring spoons

saucepan

wooden spoon

wire rack

---

5 ½ tbsp / 2 ⅔ oz / 75 g unsalted butter

♥

⅔ cup / 4 ½ oz / 125 g sugar

♥

⅓ cup / 3 fl. oz / 85 ml honey

♥

2 ¾ cups / 8 oz / 225 g rolled oats

♥

⅔ cup / 3 ½ oz / 100 g raisins

♥

2 small apples, finely chopped

1 Melt the butter, sugar, and honey in a pan over a low heat, stirring gently.

2 Take the pan off the heat and stir in the oats, raisins, and chopped apple.

3 Spoon the mixture onto the sheet and press down with the back of a spoon. Bake for 15–20 minutes until golden brown.

"Cool on a wire rack, then cut into cute slices."

choccy apples

Line a tray with wax paper.

1 Push a lollipop stick into each apple.

2 Melt the chocolate, then dip the apple into the chocolate and make sure it is completely covered.

Makes 6

You will need

tray
wax paper
measuring cups / scale
6 lollipop sticks
microwave-safe bowl
spoon

6 small sweet
apples, washed

♥

2 ¼ cups / 14 oz / 400 g
milk, white, or dark
baking chocolate

♥

3 ½ oz / 100 g
sprinkles, nuts, or
mini marshmallows

3 Shake any drips back into the bowl, wait 5 seconds, then dip the coated apple into the sprinkles, nuts, or marshmallows and leave on the tray to dry.

Cutie pies

Annie the Apple Pie Fairy

Makes
12 You will need

cupcake tray

measuring cups / scale

measuring spoons

rolling pin

3 in (8 cm) fluted
cookie cutter

small heart-shaped
cookie cutter

pastry brush

medium bowl

teaspoon

wire rack

Preheat the oven
to 375°F / 190°C
and grease the tray
with butter.

1 tbsp unsalted butter
♥
1 tbsp all-purpose flour
♥
12 ⅓ oz / 350 g
ready-made
shortcrust pastry
♥
1 tbsp milk
♥
1 tbsp brown sugar
♥
2 medium-sized
eating apples,
finely chopped
♥
2 tbsp sugar
♥
1 ¼ cups / 3 ½ oz / 100 g
granola

58

1

Roll the pastry on a floured surface. Cut out 12 circles and put them in the tray.

2

Cut out 12 hearts. Brush them with a little milk and sprinkle them with brown sugar. Then leave to one side.

3

Mix the chopped apples and sugar in a bowl.

4

Put a teaspoon of mix in each pastry cup and sprinkle with a little granola, then place a pastry heart on top.

"Bake for 25-30 minutes until golden brown, then cool on a wire rack."

Twinkly treats

Preheat the oven to 375°F / 190°C and line a baking sheet with wax paper.

Makes 16

You will need

baking sheet

wax paper

measuring cups / scale

measuring spoons

large bowl

sifter

rolling pin

2 in (5 cm) round cookie cutter

lollipop stick

wire rack

1 ½ in (4 cm) fluted cookie cutter

knife

ribbon

¾ cup / 2 ⅔ oz / 75 g all-purpose flour

♥

½ stick / 1 ¾ oz / 50 g unsalted butter

♥

2 tbsp sugar

♥

5 ⅓ oz / 150 g white fondant icing

♥

2 tbsp powdered sugar icing (see p13)

♥

1 cup / 7 oz / 200 g sugar-coated chocolates

1 Breadcrumb the flour and butter, add the sugar, and mix.

2 Shape into a ball and roll out the dough on a floured surface.

3 Cut out 12 shapes with the round cutter, put them on the sheet, and bake for 15–18 minutes until golden.

4 As soon as they come out, make a hole in the top of each cookie with a lollipop stick and cool on a wire rack.

5 Roll out the fondant icing and cut out 12 shapes with the fluted cutter.

6 Put a dab of powdered sugar icing on the top of a cookie and stick the fondant icing shape to it.

"Decorate the treats with sugar-coated **chocolates.**"

"Thread ribbon through the holes and hang your treats on a **tree.**"

61

Katie the Candy Cane Fairy

Candy cane crunch

Line a baking sheet with wax paper.

Makes 12

You will need

baking sheet
wax paper
measuring cups / scale
microwave-safe bowl
spoon
ziplock bag
rolling pin

2 cups / 12 oz / 340 g
dark / milk chocolate

♥

8 peppermint
candy canes

♥

2 cups / 12 oz / 340 g
white chocolate

2 Put the candy canes into the bag, seal it, then use a rolling pin to roll or smash the canes into small pieces.

3 Melt the white chocolate, then stir in ¾ of the candy cane pieces. Pour the melted white chocolate mix into the sheet.

1 Melt the dark chocolate, then pour it into the sheet and spread it evenly. Place the sheet in the fridge until the chocolate has set.

4 Sprinkle the rest of the candy canes on top and smooth down with a spoon. Place the sheet in the fridge until hard.

62

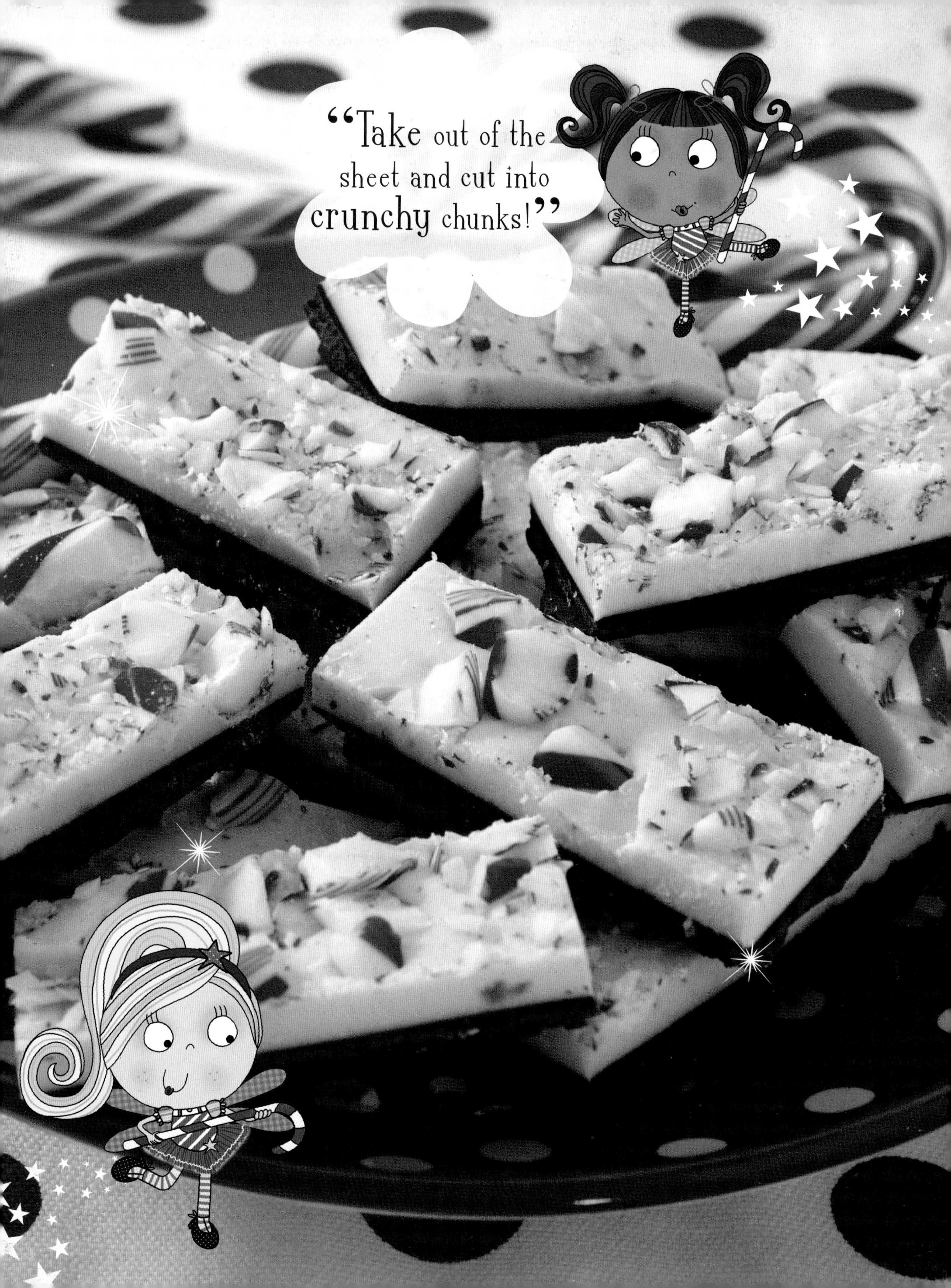
"Take out of the sheet and cut into crunchy chunks!"

Index

Concept: Joanna Bicknell
Recipes: Angela Weekes, LoveMyCake.com
Food photographer: Andy Snaith
Food stylists: Joanna Bicknell and Annie Simpson
Recipe testing: Julie Howell and Jane Manning of the Make Believe Café
Illustrations: Lara Ede
Designer: Mark Richards
Editor: Fiona Boon

Weight

Metric	Imperial	Metric	Imperial
10 g	⅓ oz	170 g	6 oz
15 g	½ oz	200 g	7 oz
20 g	¾ oz	225 g	8 oz
30 g	1 oz	255 g	9 oz
45 g	1 ½ oz	285 g	10 oz
50 g	1 ¾ oz	340 g	12 oz
60 g	2 oz	400 g	14 oz
70 g	2 ½ oz	450 g	1 lb
85 g	3 oz	500 g	1 lb 2 oz
100 g	3 ½ oz	600 g	1 lb 5 oz
115 g	4 oz	700 g	1 lb 9 oz
130 g	4 ½ oz	800 g	1 lb 12 oz
140 g	5 oz	900 g	2 lb
155 g	5 ½ oz	1 kg	2 lb 3 oz

Oven temperatures

Celsius	Fahrenheit	Gas mark
140°C	275°F	1
150°C	300°F	2
160°C	325°F	3
180°C	350°F	4
190°C	375°F	5
200°C	400°F	6
220°C	425°F	7
230°C	450°F	8
240°C	475°F	9

If you have a fan-assisted oven, reduce the temperature by at least 20 degrees.